ONE KISS

ONE KISS

MARTHE JOCELYN

orca soundings

ORCA BOOK PUBLISHERS

Published in Canada and the United States in 2025 by Orca Book Publishers.
orcabook.com

Library and Archives Canada Cataloguing in Publication
Title: One kiss / Marthe Jocelyn.
Names: Jocelyn, Marthe, author.
Series: Orca soundings.
Description: Series statement: Orca soundings
Identifiers: Canadiana (print) 20240373715 | Canadiana (ebook) 2024037388X |
ISBN 9781459840898 (softcover) | ISBN 9781459840904 (PDF) | ISBN 9781459840911 (EPUB)
Subjects: LCGFT: Novels.
Classification: LCC PS8569.O254 O527 2025 | DDC jC813/.54—dc23

Library of Congress Control Number: 2024938839

Summary: In this high-interest accessible novel for teen readers, sixteen-year-old Maya's life is thrown off-balance when the rock-star father of her best friend kisses her in the back of a limo.

Orca Book Publishers is committed to reducing the consumption of nonrenewable resources in the production of our books. We make every effort to use materials that support a sustainable future.

Orca Book Publishers gratefully acknowledges the support for its publishing programs provided by the following agencies: the Government of Canada, the Canada Council for the Arts and the Province of British Columbia through the BC Arts Council and the Book Publishing Tax Credit.

Design by Ella Collier.
Edited by Gabrielle Prendergast.
Cover illustration by Ella Collier.

Printed and bound in Canada.

28 27 26 25 • 1 2 3 4

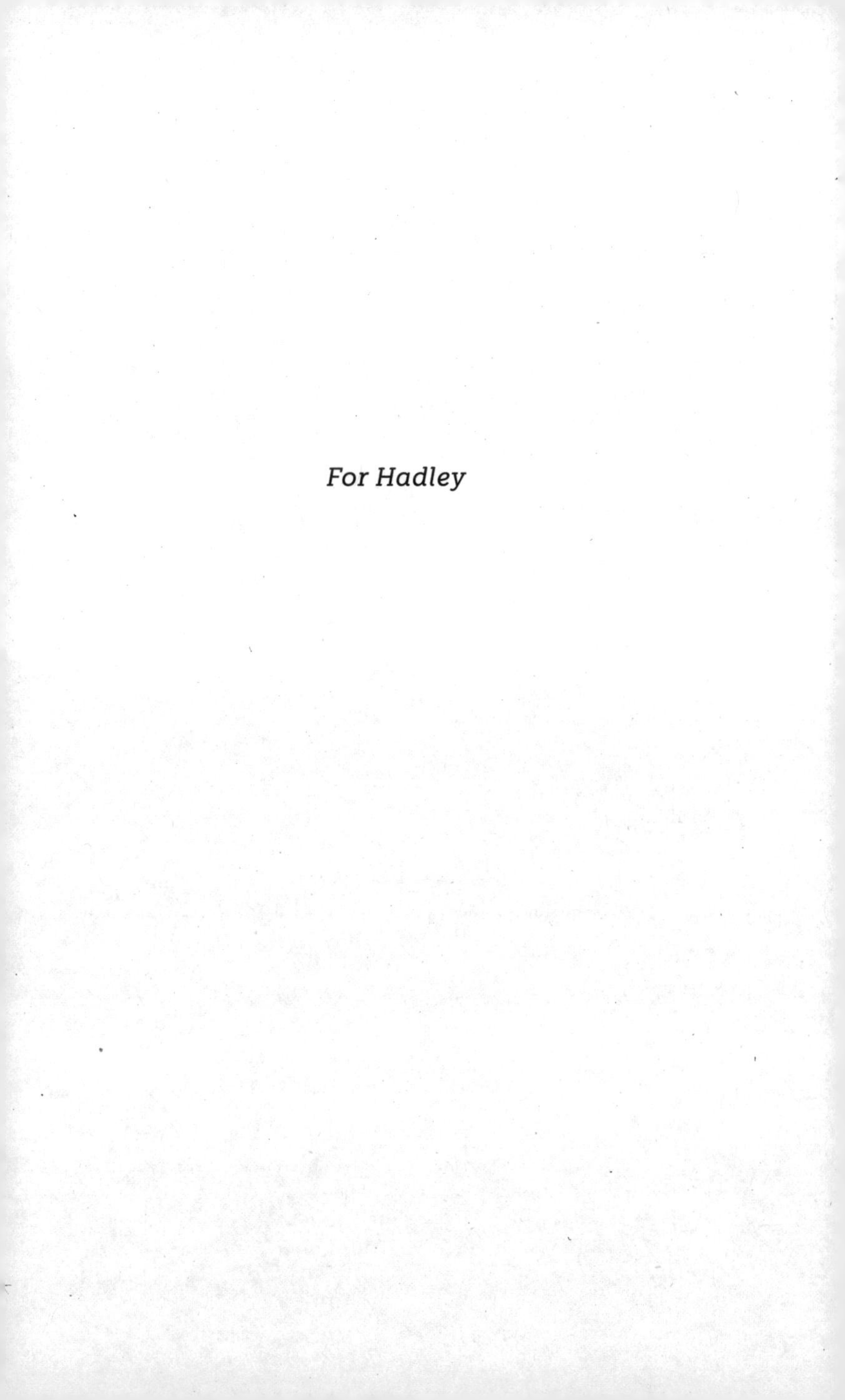

For Hadley

Chapter One

Plum always waits for me. Unless I have early swim-team practice. If it's raining, she waits in Mr. Arnott's garage. Otherwise she's at the corner. Today she is not at the corner.

I'm four minutes late. But I'm always four minutes late. Why would she leave on me this morning?

where are you? I text.

No answer.

When I get to school, Plum is with Jones and Ava beside Ava's locker. Other kids bang past. Someone's phone is jingling. Jones is checking the eleven hairs on his upper lip in Ava's locker mirror.

"Hey!" Plum grabs my arm. "Sorry, I had to come early. I forgot my phone."

"You forgot your phone?" This is *so* not likely.

The bell rings for class.

"Her dad's in town," says Ava. Her smirk is pure cat, thinking she knows the hot news before I do.

"Your dad?" I say. And quickly add, "Oh, right. Well, I guess the secret's out."

Plum grins. She likes when I cover for her. That's what a sidekick is for. I link my arm through hers and drag her away.

"He's actually here? In Toronto?" We trot toward homeroom.

"Ava was at the corner instead of you," says Plum. "She'd already read online that he arrived last night."

"With the band? Or just to see you?" He usually flies her to Berlin. He hasn't been back here since he left six years ago.

"He never even warned us. The phone started ringing at six this morning. Reporters asking if my mother's going to play on the album."

"The album?"

"That's why The Scratch is here, to record a new album. Number seven? Eight? At least three since my mom left the band."

"But why here?"

"Something about getting it done faster in Canada? So it's out before the North American tour next year? How would I know? I haven't spoken to him abou–"

We skid into room 109 and hustle to our seats. On opposite sides of the room, thanks to Mr. Thomas. He claims we talk too much.

"Miss Kenner," he says to Plum. "And Miss Delaney. So kind of you to join us. Do get comfortable."

He starts reading names in a deep voice. As if "Homeroom Attendance" is a poem. We can all see that every seat is filled. I check my phone to find out WTF is going on with Plum's dad. I manage to see that *Ross Kenner* is trending. But then Mr. Thomas gives me his famous uh-uh-uh shake of the head, so I stick the phone in my bag.

My brain is fizzing. This is hot news. We were ten when he bailed on Plum and her mom—two years before my dad bailed on me and mine. My mother, I have to say, is better off being a parent alone. My dad would do things like impose a dumb rule for no reason. Then they'd bicker. Then he'd walk out. Then Mom would make a better rule, my father would totally forget, and we'd roll along till the next time.

I learned something from watching them not like each other. Being married isn't always worth the effort.

Plum's mother, Talia, quit The Scratch right about when they got super famous. We listen to their music but mostly from the early albums. Talia might have been the best part. Whatever happened with Ross, she chose to stay behind and be a mom. Which she doesn't seem to regret.

I guess Plum misses him, but she comes back from her visits in Berlin with the best stories. Limousines, late nights, amazing new clothes. But really she doesn't talk about her father too much, even with me. Unless some idiot says "Omg your dad is dating Kristy Glenn from the *Dark Night* series?" Then she goes cold and later has to vent to me for an hour. So do *not* get gooey or ask what it's like to have a rock-star dad. That's like saying goodbye to Plum. Ava walks on thin ice in this arena. She gets away with it because we like Jones. Jones is Ava's best friend. Why, exactly, we do not know.

Forty minutes of homeroom feels like an entire day. Then biology. Then writing craft. It's lunch before Plum and I breathe the same air again. She picks up right where she left off.

"They're using a recording studio called Toast with Tea. It's downtown. We found that out from a reporter for *Pitchfork*." She pulls out her phone as we walk and turns it on. "Let's go to Pete's. I don't want to see Ava."

"You forgot your phone?" I say with a smirk.

"Ha, well, Mom said to turn it off in case the press figures out how to find me. She...you know..."

"Doesn't want the paparazzi to bother you," I say.

"Plus I didn't want Ava to see I had no texts from my dad. I mean, why didn't he let me know he's coming?" The phone lights up as it comes back to life. "Oh, wait."

She shows me the screen. A ribbon of notifications. Texts and missed calls. One from her mom, a couple from Eddie, but most from Ross.

She calls her dad Ross. Even when she was little, she never called him Daddy.

"Who's Eddie again?" I ask.

"Works for Ross," says Plum. "Good to know he's still around. Should I call my dad or send him a text? All of his just say 'call me.'"

"Maybe check with your mom? See what she knows?"

"You're so smart, Maya my darlin'." She makes a kissy sound in my direction and clicks her mother's number. "Order me fries," she whispers.

"With gravy," we say together.

"Hi, Mom," says Plum.

I turn to order at the window of the fry van.

"...no, I'm with Maya. Ross called but my phone was off, like you told me...no, no strange numbers, no reporters...Oh, ugh! So you're blocking them all...But did you talk to Ross?" She listens. Nods, murmurs uh-huh. Then "Okay, yeah, I'll let you know what he says."

Pete pushes two paper boats of fries across the counter. Plum digs in her pocket for money. She keeps the phone to her ear. She always pays. She's not rich. Not like her dad. But she has more than I do.

"'Kay, I'm going to eat. Bye, Mom. Not just fries, I promise. Oh, Maya says hi."

Plum hits *end* and takes her fries. "Mom says hi back." She adds ketchup on top of the gravy. We disagree about this. But today I don't comment. We sit on a wall to eat our fries.

"So? What did she say?"

"He called her to say hi. He wants to see me," says Plum. "Which, of course he does. It's almost a year since I went over there for Christmas."

"But...?" I can hear the *but* waiting to come out.

"Honestly?" Her voice drops to a whisper. "I'm a little nervous. Isn't that sad? It feels not normal, him being here."

"You chat with him most months. You've had some Zoom calls."

"Yeah, but it's always short. He's never alone. It's not really real."

"Realer than the ghost of Mr. Stephen Delaney," I say. Plum smiles and lays her head on my shoulder for a second.

My dad is not actually a ghost. He's still alive somewhere. Making support payments on time, but not part of life as I know it. To copy Plum, when we were maybe eleven, I called him by his name one time.

"Stephen," I said. "Will you please pass the ketchup?"

My mother laughed, but my dad did not. "Do I look like a rock star?" he said. "Am I wearing a T-shirt with my muscles hanging out?"

I shook my head no. I wasn't sure he had any muscles. Did men at desks grow muscles?

"To you," he said, "my name is Dad."

Except when he decided not to be and took off about a year later. I've talked with him way less than Plum has with Ross. Has he ever been in town and not told me? I'd rather not know.

"Just call him!" I say.

She looks at me, hazel eyes kind of shiny. I'm trying to read her, but I think she already said it. She's excited to see him, obviously. Texting only goes so far. And their texts are about gossip mostly, not real life.

So on her home turf, she's on edge. As if he's an invader somehow. When she goes to Berlin she feels like a jet-setter. She can slip into his world and be whoever. Here I know her better than he does. We're just us, living a plain old life.

Will that be cool enough for rock star Ross Kenner?

Chapter Two

"Call him before the bell rings," I say. "Then you'll know."

"Hi," she says into the phone. Her voice croaks. "Hi, Ross. It's Plum."

People always want to know why Plum is named Plum. She says, "Better than Apple."

She smiles a big, relieved smile. He must be saying something sweet. That's what I remember from when we were kids. He was always playful as a dad.

Not hung up on rules or schedules or whether something was *appropriate.* I bet he drove the other parents nuts. For sure my dad thought he was a weirdo, because Dad's babysitting technique was to make us wash the porch steps or rake the lawn.

Ross took us out for what he called mystery missions. We'd wade in public fountains or walk on the top of walls. We ate marshmallows as snacks. I think I missed Ross more than Mr. Stephen Delaney when he left, because at least Ross was fun.

"Tonight?" says Plum. "Where?" She wags her hand wildly, making a writing motion. I smooth out a napkin. She uses her lip pencil.

Hot Sam's, she scrawls. Like smears of blood on the napkin. The name of a street. Then *7 p.m.*

"I'll ask Maya," says Plum. "See you later." She ends the call. She looks at me, beaming. "He sounds just like himself," she says. "He asked about you. He said—"

"Who said what?" Jones slings an arm around my shoulder. I'd been busy watching Plum. And suddenly Jones and Ava are here.

"Just my dad." Plum's shoulders lift and fall. A perfect display of boredom. "I'm meeting him later." The napkin disappears into her pocket.

Ava's eyes follow it. "Do you think Kristy Glenn will be there too?"

I frown at her, and Jones rams an elbow into her side. But Plum is glowing. She just talked to her dad and doesn't get prickly.

"Not sure their thing is that big a deal," she says. "For Kristy to fly in." As if her father confides in her about his love life. But maybe tonight she'll get the scoop.

So off we all go to our various thrilling classes. And I'm still wondering what Plum told Ross she'd ask me.

I don't find out until halfway through PE.

We're "warming up" with a one-kilometer run around the track. *Run* being a generous term for what most of us are doing. It's the last class of the day. As long as we're moving, Ms. Foley doesn't care.

"I'm meeting him for dinner," says Plum. "He said to invite you too. Maybe he gets that I'll be nervous? That I might want a friend?"

"How about I say I can't make it till, like, dessert?" I say. "Then you'll have time alone first."

"You're the best," says Plum. "Just as thoughtful as you are pretty." That part she says in a cheesy grandma's voice. I pretend to retch.

"Keep moving," calls Ms. Foley. "This is not gossip hour."

Oh, but it kind of is. Word about Plum's dad being in town has buzzed through the school. Usually kids are pretty chill about him being lead singer in a famous band. But now that he's in this very city? We notice heads turning as we leave at the end of the day. We hear Plum's name and Ross's repeated in whispers. A couple of kids even take pictures. For sure Plum is photo worthy. Creamy gold skin, thanks to her Indonesian grandmother. Thick black hair and her dad's famous hazel-green eyes.

"How does Talia feel?" I ask. "About you seeing Ross and all the weird attention?"

"Mom's fine," Plum says. "She knows I miss him. Seeing him is better than texting. And she knows better than anyone how weird the weirdness can be. That's why she quit The Scratch. So I didn't have to grow up with—" She breaks off to yell, "Hey, piss off with the phones!"

A couple of ninth graders have been click-click-clicking. But now they piss off.

"Yeesh," says Plum. "What if Ross lived here instead of Berlin and this was my life?"

"It would get old really fast," I agree. "Plus who wants to be famous for something you had no control over?"

Plum nods. "All I did was get born."

She gives me the address of the place for dinner. I manage not to ask what she's wearing. She always looks amazing. I feel a bit wishy-washy next to her. She always knows exactly what she thinks about things. It sometimes takes me a day to come up with my own opinion. She is the star of any room she's in, and I'm the one standing by the door, ready to leave. She'd tell me not to be an idiot because I'm the one with the long legs and long hair, but that sort of makes it worse. "Statuesque" she calls me, even though standing up straight is one of my biggest challenges.

But tonight? I want to be there for Plum. And I'm super curious to see Ross too. I'll even wear my boots with heels.

At home my mother is not thrilled with our plans.

"It's a school night," she says. "And where is this place? Taking teenage girls to some dive on Spadina after dark? Typical Ross."

"Mom! Plum's dad hasn't been here in six years! Can't you just be happy for her?"

"Of course I'm happy for her. I'd be even happier if Ross made a better plan. Less about what works for him. More about spending time with her."

"He's going to spend time with her! That's why I'm going later. They're meeting at seven and I'm showing up at eight."

Mom just sighs. Ross and Talia used to be good friends with my parents, starting when Plum and I were in kindergarten. Mom has mixed feelings about Ross. She sees why he's a star. He's handsome. A famous rebel. But I'm guessing there are a few chapters of history. My mother is not one to dish dirt, so who really knows? It's pretty clear she thinks he is not to be trusted. That Ross is all about Ross.

"Do I wear it up or down?" I'm brushing my hair, trying to distract her.

"Down," she says. "And do up another button."

I smile at her and do up the button. I'm wearing black, but the shirt is a bit slinky and the skirt is a bit short. I know Mom is dying to tell me to put on, like, a snowsuit.

A text comes in from Plum. **already a crowd here. no time alone anyway. come sooner.**

Poor Plum! Having to share her dad on their very first night!

"Typical Ross," says my mother again when I tell her. "Why are famous people so afraid of being alone? They seem to live in a crowd all the time!"

"Bye, Mom!"

I smear on another dab of lip balm. I grab my bag and my phone, and race to the rescue.

Chapter Three

Hot Sam's is one of those places I've passed a million times but never entered. From a streetcar, it looks like a seedy old tavern, out of place in a row of Chinese restaurants. The name etched into the old sign on the front reads *Flannagan's Bar*. Plum warned me about that. Hot Sam's is the secret alias.

I'm pretty sure a bouncer is not one of the regular features. But tonight there's a rock star inside. A big man stands in front of the door. He has on a dark turtleneck sweater and a leather jacket. His bald head gleams under the streetlights. He is earning his pay, because the crowd is so big it spills into the road.

A few of the people are locals, on their way home from work or picking up takeout. They're probably wondering what the hell is going on. This busy street is usually in motion. Right now it's clogged. A rope barricade has been set up, keeping back a huge gaggle of girls and women who are waving and calling out. Some of them have signs. Like *WE HEART ROSS K!* and *Scratch My Itch!!* So dumb.

Then there's a cluster of people holding cameras with crazy-long lenses. The dread reporters. The scene looks like a clip from the news. Or part of an episode about a movie star.

This is the weirdness Plum's mother gave up her career to avoid. She traded millions of dollars for not being followed or watched.

I start out being polite, asking people to please let me through. Soon I'm squeezing and pushing my way past. Finally I get to the bald leather guy. He's looking over my head, scanning the crowd.

"Hello," I say. He doesn't even meet my eyes. I have to shout a little for him to hear me. "Um, excuse me?"

He checks me out for half a second.

"I'm meeting the Ross Kenner party inside," I explain.

One of his eyebrows flicks up. His mouth might have twitched into the hint of a smile.

"Nice try, kid," he says. "But no. Step back, please."

"For real," I say. "I'm friends with Plum! His daughter!"

He raises a palm to show that my pleading is pointless. He goes back to ignoring me.

Now what?

i'm outside, I text to Plum. **bouncer won't let me in. you're too famous.**

I hope she's checking her phone. The bouncer juts his chin toward the rope. He wants me to join the hundred fans behind it. I shuffle over two steps. A woman scowls at me. The rope is pressing into her gut below the words on her T-shirt: *Ross is Boss!!*

"No way you're getting in front of me," she says. "I left work early to be here."

My phone vibrates.

wait a sec, writes Plum. **we'll get you.**

Will it really be a second? I stay where I am.

The bouncer is now leaning against the door of Hot Sam's. Arms crossed over his chest. He suddenly jumps and spins around. The door opens a crack. I hope it's Plum on the other side. Or a waiter to be my escort. The bouncer talks through the gap. Shakes his head. Then he puts up his hands, like he's giving up. He backs away from the door as it opens.

A crazy clamor erupts before I see why. But I can guess. The air swells with shouts and whistles. Someone screams. Cameras click wildly. Ross Kenner himself has stepped through the door. He offers a friendly wave to the crowd.

He has one of those faces that belongs on the cover of a romance novel. Sharp cheekbones and a dimple in the right cheek. Crinkles around his eyes. Tawny skin and dark hair. His hair is famous for being a mess of curls. Plum is jealous because hers is straw straight. But Ross is showing off a new haircut. Short except for a few curls that dangle over his eyes.

Ross shouts into the leather guy's ear. The leather guy turns to look at me. I raise my hand in a dumb wave. *Ha,* I'm thinking. *Didn't believe me, eh? Your job would have been so much easier if you'd just let me in.* Then I realize he knew exactly where I was. I guess he kept a bodyguard's eye on me in case I was a wack job.

Ross spots me and strolls over. The crowd explodes. The bouncer is right behind but not quick enough. Ross has one hand up, shielding his face from flashing cameras. His other hand reaches for mine.

"Hey, darlin'!" somebody shouts. One of the reporters. "Look over here!"

The bouncer swings open the door. Ross throws an arm over my shoulder. Weirdly, we seem to be the same height. Last time I saw him, he was, you know, as tall as a father. There's a burst of clicking and flashing. The door closes behind us.

Inside, we're in a tiny space hung with velvet curtains. An old chandelier dangles above our heads. It casts hardly any light but lots of ghostly shadows. In winter this velvet nook stops icy wind from blowing into the bar. For a second we're alone in what is almost a closet.

"Wow, thanks," I say. "That was crazy."

"Another day, another frenzied crowd," says Ross. His voice is deep and warm. Do I remember it from my childhood? He always read stories aloud during sleepovers. Or do I know his voice from songs and YouTube interviews?

"Little Maya!" He pats my arm, catching my hair in his fingers for a second. "Look at you, all grown up."

Chapter Four

Plum yanks open the velvet curtain. I throw my arms around her as if we've been apart three weeks instead of three hours. I'd almost done the same thing with Ross! I'd been thinking of Plum this whole day, reuniting with her dad. Not what it might be like for *me* to see Ross again. I guess I've missed him too. And here he is, a weird blend of familiar and rock-star hot. Definitely not a dad.

Plum pulls me through the busy bar area. Then through the busy restaurant. Ross is right behind us.

All the patrons have raised phones. I lift my chin and casually toss back my hair. I straighten my shoulders. This must be what it's like to be famous. Strangers are always watching.

At the back, next to the kitchen, is another velvet curtain. Plum pulls it aside to reveal a private dining room. Ta-da! Like the opening of a new act. Two handsome men and a scary-looking woman are at the table. The scene is set. Deep-red walls. Flickering candles in giant glass jars. Golden bubbly wine in tall skinny glasses. The woman's diamond necklace twinkles. They all look up with big smiles.

"Everyone," says Plum. "This is Maya." We plunk into chairs.

They all say hello.

"Did you give the fans a thrill out there?" the woman asks Ross. She has blazing-red hair and chalk-white skin. On purpose. As if she has baby powder in her compact.

Plum points at each. "Bella is my dad's manager. Milan and Eddie just got married. Like, a week ago. What happened to the others?"

"Jem and Harry have gone," says Eddie. "They left through the kitchen. As will we."

Eddie is Ross's assistant. Italian? Greek? Nice brown eyes that smile at me. His scruff is not quite a beard. His handsome husband looks Indian, with shiny black hair pulled back in a ponytail.

"I do love escapes through kitchens," says Ross. He is sitting at the head of the table. The server goes to fill his tall glass. Her name tag says *DEB*. She is slim and East Asian. Her hair is up in a fab knot.

"Debbie, darlin', I'll just have water. But give some to the girls." Ross waves toward Plum and me.

I'm still catching my breath from the mob scene outside. And now Deb is pouring bubbly wine into a glass for Plum. Then one for me. My eyes meet Plum's. My mom would flip. She'd say, *Typical Ross, serving alcohol to teenagers.*

Milan is next to me. He leans in to whisper.

"No law says you have to drink it." He has an English accent. I take a sip, and it's delicious.

"Better than the stuff at Ava's party," says Plum. They all laugh. I guess it's something fancy.

Bella turns to Plum. "Honey, your mother."

Not a question, just "your mother." Plum's eyes cut over to Ross.

"Did she tell you?" Bella's voice booms in the small room. "We begged her to be part of this album."

I can tell that Plum did not know this. But Ross butts in.

"Nobody begged," he says. "Bella asked. Talia said no. End of story."

The curtain opens and Deb pushes in a trolley stacked with platters. The room fills with the best smells, all of us gasping at the feast Deb is serving.

"We ordered one of everything on the menu," says Ross, "so we'll know what we like best for next time."

A few minutes go by while we eat. No problem sampling every dish. I notice Ross is eating only endives with pomegranate seeds.

Then Bella tries the chit-chat thing again. “Maya, what’s your favorite Scratch song?”

On the spot or what? How do I answer? My favorite? In front of everybody? In front of Ross? Deep breath. I take a sip of water. *Be cool.*

“When we were little,” I say, “Plum and I went to rehearsal sometimes. Once, I remember—we were about nine?—we sat on the floor and played checkers.”

Plum says, “I remember that!”

“The band was working on a song. They played it over and over, with little variations each time.”

They’re all listening. I can feel Ross watching me. Am I babbling? I focus on telling it to Bella.

“Talia tried multiple riffs on the violin. Ross kept tweaking the words.”

“We wanted to sing along,” Plum says, “but the song kept changing.”

"Until suddenly it was perfect," I say. "And we totally thought we'd helped a song get born. That one is my favorite. 'Until Forever, Pretty Girl.'"

"We wrote it for Plum," says Ross.

"That's the story, anyway," says Plum. Ross looks at her. She lifts her glass to drain it. The waiter is holding the prosecco bottle, ready for a refill.

"Still our number one download," Eddie says. "That day's hard work probably paid for tonight's dinner." They all laugh again, even though it's not that funny. It probably paid for every holiday Plum has ever had in Berlin and plenty more.

"And what do you do outside of school?" asks Milan.

"Maya's a swimmer," says Plum, because I would never.

"A swimmer!" says Ross. "Make those legs work, eh?"

He noticed my legs? I guess I've always been taller than Plum. *Thanks, heels.*

"And she's helping the director for the school musical," says Plum.

"Plum's going to be the star," I say, because *she* would never. "Plum can really sing."

"Can you?" Ross sits up straight, eyes locked on Plum. How does he not know this?

"She's really good," I say.

Plum kicks me. I stop talking.

"I'd love to hear you," says Ross. His voice has changed. From lazy to excited and curious.

I tap Plum's arm, mouthing *Sorry*. She looks away. Ouch.

I say no to more prosecco. I say no to more food too, even though I could eat for an hour. But no one else has seconds, let alone thirds. To them it's normal to order one of everything just to taste.

One of five cell phones on the table lights up. It vibrates and also makes the sound of crickets. Ross looks at the screen. He turns the phone face down and looks at Eddie. Eddie raises his eyebrows, asking a question. They're like Plum and me. Talking without talking. Ross nods with a shrug. Eddie shrugs back.

I look at Plum. She rolls her eyes. My heart skips. I am forgiven. And we're thinking the same thing. Kristy Glenn, the famous actress, is calling from New York. Kristy Glenn is clearly not about to be Plum's stepmother.

"Have we paid?" Ross says. Eddie nods. Chairs shift, people stand. I wish I could take home a doggy bag, but I don't think celebrities do that. Plum pulls her backpack from under her chair.

"Sorry about before," I whisper. "Why don't you want him to know that you—"

"Shh." She's staying in Ross's suite at the hotel. The men pocket their phones. Bella has a handbag made of what looks like a chain-link fence.

Ross salutes the chef as we head to the back door. A pimply dishwasher takes a photo. Deb the server calls out a thanks for the big tip. We all smile and wave. Right this minute I feel famous. As if I have a life that requires sneaking out through a kitchen.

Two taxis and a black SUV limo thing are waiting outside. Bella takes the first taxi. Eddie and Milan scoop me into theirs. I wink at Plum before she gets into the SUV with her dad. She'll be alone with him at last.

"Can't we just go to bed?" Milan says to Eddie.

"Sorry, babe," says Eddie. "I'm beat too. But people are coming to Ross's suite at the hotel. If I don't show up, he'll call nine times before dawn."

Milan sighs and shuts his eyes.

Is every night like this?

"We'll drop Maya," says Eddie. "We'll pick up the pistachio ice cream he's so crazy for. Then back to the hotel."

"The party just keeps going?" I ask. Poor Plum! So much for father-daughter bonding.

Milan laughs, his eyes still closed. "The party never ends."

"He only does this when they're recording," says Eddie. "Ross is a total health nut if he's on a concert tour. He has to stay fit."

"Especially now that he's thirty-seven," says Milan. "Downhill from here."

"Also why he looks so good," says Eddie.

It's true—Ross does look pretty good.

Milan opens his eyes to fake-glare at his husband.

"Not as good as you, babe," says Eddie.

I clear my throat. They both laugh. They're totally nice guys.

"Right now they're in the studio all day," Eddie explains. "Ross hardly sleeps. He's not a drinker. He doesn't smoke or do drugs. But he likes to stay up all night, like a teenager. Says it keeps him loose. He likes when the microphone picks up gravel in his voice. Late-night gravel."

"A true artiste," says Milan. Sarcastic, but I can tell they're all buddies.

We turn onto my block.

The taxi driver calls out, “Left side or right?”

“Right,” I say. “Thank you.”

Eddie hops out. He comes around and opens my door. As if I’m the celebrity.

My mother is standing on the porch before I’m halfway up the walk.

Chapter Five

It's just starting to drizzle next morning. And surprise! Plum is on the corner.

"What are you doing here?" I say. "I thought you were taking the day off! Floating in the hotel pool. Having your nails done."

She looks awful. Not that Plum ever looks truly awful. But she has circles as dark as bruises under her eyes.

"As if," she mutters. "I didn't even sleep there."

"Why not?"

"Bella was already in the suite when we showed up. We were late because Ross was mobbed in the lobby. By the time we made it upstairs, the room-service guy was rolling in a trolley. Ice and drinks and jalapeño poppers or whatever."

She shudders. "I couldn't face it. I wanted to sleep in my own bed. Eddie put me in a taxi. My mother was thrilled. Except she could tell I'd been drinking."

"Only nine proseccos," I joke. "What about the limo ride?" Meaning the few minutes she'd been alone with her dad.

"Ha ha," she says. "We're in the car *one second.* And he pulls out his phone to call Kristy Glenn." I hear a little crack in her voice. "He was like, 'I'd better get this out of the way or I'll be in big trouble.'"

"Oh, Plum."

"Right? I mean, you're a grown man, you dick! We see each other once a year and—" She stops.

Ava is standing in front of the fruit market. Plum lowers her voice. "Don't tell anyone, I beg of you."

"Obviously," I say.

"We had the most amazing night, okay?"

"We sure did." This happens to be totally true for me. Drinking prosecco. Deb the server fluttering around. The sesame braised mushrooms. The fried artichoke. Hanging out with Eddie and Milan. The whole behind-the-scenes glamor thing. Seeing Ross again.

Jones comes out of the market, holding his morning banana and a bag of pretzels. Ava waves her phone at us.

"You saw your dad!" she cries.

Plum pulls up a radiant smile. "Yup."

"And what the hell, Maya?" Ava waves her phone again. "You're a paparazzi darling!" Her big smile can't hide the tremor of envy in her voice.

"What?"

"Our very own very tall little Maya," says Jones. "Trending!" He shows us the photo on his screen. "Except nobody knows who you are."

Outside Hot Sam's. Ross Kenner's hand and my hand are sort of reaching for each other. The bouncer is right behind Ross. His face looks pissed.

"The bald guy wouldn't let me in," I say. "I tried to tell him I was meeting Plum, but—"

"It was nuts out there," says Plum. "I think Bella leaked the dinner plan. They do that all the time. You know, to ramp up the buzz."

"They do?" I feel so dumb.

"It's a big game to them. Managers just want to sell the product, right?"

"And the product is your dad," says Jones. "Pretty hot product, if you don't mind me saying."

He's right. And Ross in person is even hotter than Ross on a poster. Not that I would ever say that out loud.

Plum laughs and gives Jones a push. "He's an old man."

"No less hot for that," says Jones.

"Find a boy your own age," says Plum. "My dad's assistant, Eddie, has such a cute husband. Right, Maya?"

"Fact," I say. "Second fact, one minute till the bell." Time to forget about famous fathers. And paparazzi. And grown-ups who take taxis to get ice cream.

Even the teachers seem to know. Mr. Thomas makes a point of asking Plum if she read the homework chapter. And then he asks me. Checking up on us, with Plum's dad in town and my photo trending. As if I ever thought I'd say those words—*my photo trending*. How weird is that? The drama teacher, Mr. Forest, asks Plum to do a major number for Cabaret Night next spring. *And* he asks me to be his assistant director. And then Madame Lacroix—who never smiles—smiles at me! The effort makes her top lip pucker like tissue paper.

It's almost funny, like fame is contagious.

It's still raining at lunchtime. This means we're stuck in the cafeteria. Kids Plum doesn't even know find reasons to brush against her in the lineup for food. Ava and Jones come to sit with us. Ava is humming a Scratch hit called "Tumble Me." As if she doesn't realize.

"Could you not?" Plum says.

"Touchy," says Ava. She turns to me. "What was he wearing, Maya? Tight tee or—"

"Ava," says Jones.

Plum's face is a blank screen. "You do know my parents are both real people in my life?" she says. "Not characters on a reality show?"

A flush creeps up Ava's neck. I am so happy not to be her right now.

"Plus? My parents are friends. We're all pals," Plum says. "My father purposely booked the studio in Toronto to spend time with us. Everything is beautiful, got it?"

Ava nods. Plum crushes her sandwich paper into a ball. She scrapes her chair back and stands.

"Coming?" she says to me.

My eyes meet Jones's. I make a face to tell him *yikes* and *you're a good guy* in the same second.

Plum scoops up her bag, and I follow.

"I guess I could have smiled while I was talking happy families," says Plum.

"Mm-hmm," I say.

We're passing the staff room. The school secretary, Mouth-Breather Ms. Carlaw, waves at Plum.

"Nice that your dad is here for a visit!" she calls out.

"Don't visits involve talking to each other?" murmurs Plum, pulling out her phone.

"That's the usual idea," I agree. I wish she'd had as much fun as I did last night. But I got what I wanted. A little taste of the rock-star life. Plum got the opposite of what she wanted, which was dinner alone with her father. And what did Ross want?

"Maybe he wants to show you off to his people," I say. "Maybe he doesn't know how to be with you alone. Maybe he's nervous too!"

Plum sighs and turns her screen for me to see a text from Ross.

Let's do it again! Same place, same time! Bring Maya!

Chapter Six

By the end of the day, Plum is revved back up to see her dad. I just want to sit in that room again, eating delicious snacks and feeling *in* with Ross and his pals.

No surprise, my mom says no.

"Two school nights, back-to-back? Think again, young lady."

Luckily, Plum and I expected this problem. She came home with me for this very reason.

"Patty?" says Plum, in a voice as sweet as her name. "Here's the thing. I get to see my dad for only a week or two each year. Our bonding thing is a little rusty, you know?"

"Spending time together is wonderful for you," my mother says. "I wish it could happen more often."

"Yeah," says Plum. "Except Ross has people around him all the time. You know how that is. His manager, his assistant, someone to pour his citrus water. If Maya doesn't come, I'm stranded. Alone in a crowd, you know? I *need* her there."

Plum is playing this exactly right. Mom thinks Ross should be ashamed of himself. Maybe because she's so mad at my own father, who is also not a great example of the perfect parent with his disappearing act and one-line birthday cards.

She sighs. A good sign.

Plum reads her too. "I'll tell Ross we can't stay

out late," she says. "Maya and I will come home together in the taxi."

"Do you have homework?" says Mom.

"The smallest paragraph of French to translate," I tell her. "We thought *maaay*be we could do it together? While we get dressed? At Plum's?"

"This one time," says Mom.

We manage not to squeal, but we do hug her.

"Thank you!! Thank you!!"

We hear a screeching violin as we come up the drive. No way is it Talia playing.

"Student," says Plum. "Let's go around back."

Their front room has been made into a music room. That's where Talia practices. Also where she teaches. Plum never goes in there. The kitchen is our main place to hang out. The breakfast nook is all windows and a million plants. Built-in benches with cushions.

We make toast with peanut butter. We do our French at the table. I lied to my mom about how much. Ugh. But we finish before Talia comes in. She gulps down a glass of water.

"One more student," she says. "I was thinking pad Thai for supper. Can you stay, Maya?"

"Oh, I love your pad Thai!" I say.

"But," says Plum, "we're meeting Dad."

"Pad Thai next time," I say.

Talia sighs. Finishes her water. "Better you than me." She goes back to her music room.

We make a good team, Plum and me. Everyone needs a mom-buddy to take the pressure off. Kind of like good cop, bad cop.

I borrow a dress from Plum. It's blazing green. And shorter on me than it maybe should be. I'm taller than she is by three inches. The square neckline makes my collarbones look awesome. We try on a bunch of makeup—dark lipstick and bold eyeliner.

We look older. And too weird. We wash it off. Then we brush on a little mascara and a smooch of lip balm.

Talia calls a Lyft to take us to Hot Sam's. This is pretty nice, since she's already tired of the whole Ross-in-town thing.

"What's Eddie's husband like?" It's the only thing she wants to know. Eddie was with The Scratch—as a roadie—when Talia played in the band.

"He's so cool." I'm the expert on Milan, thanks to our twelve-minute taxi ride.

Talia's eyes sweep us up and down. "You're rocking Plum's dress," she says. "Have fun, girls. Be smart."

Outside the restaurant, the crowd is a little bigger than it was last night. The same bouncer says hi and lets us in, no problem.

"His nickname is Bilbo," Plum tells me. "Dad gave him a hundred-dollar tip last night."

We go through the bar. We get to the velvet curtain in front of the private room. Plum grabs my arm.

"I mean it about leaving early," she whispers.

I say okay, but I'm hoping we don't have to. Maybe Ross will win her over and Plum will want to stay.

Chapter Seven

Inside are Milan and Eddie, Bella, Ross and the drummer, named Jem. Ross's face lights up when we come in. He jumps to his feet, knocking his chair against Deb the server. He slings an arm around Plum and kisses her cheek. He kisses *my* cheek. For some reason I giggle. Why am I giggling? He has an arm around me too.

"Look at my pretty girls," he says to Jem. As if we're both his kids.

Jem says how cool it is to meet us. He is a Black guy from Germany. His smile is big. His accent is strong. He has only been with The Scratch for a year and never knew Talia.

Ross makes Bella move so Plum can sit next to him. I'm between Bella and Milan.

Things unfold along the same lines as last night. Same servers, same company, more delicious food. A whole platter of deep-fried artichokes. A dip made from roasted red peppers. And more prosecco. The band recorded a whole song today. That doesn't happen often, so they're happy. But tired too. Energy is low.

Eddie is mostly on his phone. Bella is mostly on her phone. Milan does magic tricks as if we're five. He makes stuff vanish under his napkin. Then up his sleeve. Jem and Ross have a long chat about Jem's new drumsticks. Plum bugs her eyes at me, like, *this is boring*. And it kind of is—except these guys are rock stars! We're on the inside of the clockwork. Jones and Ava and a million other people would die to be in this room.

Then Ross asks Plum if she wants to visit the studio tomorrow. Plum stares at him.

"I've got school," she says.

Ross shrugs, like, *who cares*? A grin spreads across Plum's face.

"I'd love to!" she says.

Ross crinkles his famous eyes. Score! He looks pleased with himself.

"We can put you on tape," he says. "Have a listen."

Plum glances my way. She wants to be chill, but she is stoked.

I'm wishing hard that I'd get invited too. That Plum and I together could skip school and choose cool stuff to wear—to a recording studio! I wish that I could sing.

None of that is going to happen.

"Let's go." Ross stands up. We all grab our stuff and follow Eddie. We parade through the kitchen. Jem peels off to catch a cab. Ross points Plum and me to his limo.

"What happened to Lenny?" Ross asks the driver, a chunky white guy wearing an open-collar white shirt. Dark curly hair almost crawls up his neck.

"Lenny got called away. I'm the sub." He taps his chest. "Fred. At your service."

Fred opens the car door, and we climb in.

"Lenny's my guy," Ross mutters.

A ribbon of teeny pin lights runs around the roof inside. The interior smells like new leather. The music is Beyoncé.

Ross taps on the divider. The black glass slides open.

"Cut the noise," says Ross. The song instantly stops. The window slides shut. We're sealed in a black-leather pod, like we're going to space.

Because of one-way streets, we come to Plum's house before mine. The driver starts to get out, but Ross waves him off.

"I've got this," he says.

Fred slips back into the front seat. Ross hops out to hold the door for Plum. I'm wondering why we didn't go around the block and drop me off first. Plum's dad time cut short again. At least she's having a day in the studio tomorrow.

I lean back in the dark, against the little leather headrest.

"Are you coming in to say hey to Mom?" Plum asks Ross as she climbs out.

"Not tonight. We're having lunch on Sunday," he says.

"You *are*?" That's all I hear. They go up the walk. Ross stands for a second, looking at the house. It used to be his. Before he got the fancy townhouse in Berlin. But maybe sometimes he misses the green door or the hammock? Mowing the lawn? Having a family? Probably not. Everyone says Berlin is amazing.

Plus...rock star.

Ross comes back. He tells Fred my address again. Gets in and sits in the spot Plum just left. Right next to me. He pulls the door shut. The limo glides away from the curb, making no noise at all. Our little pod is totally quiet. My brain is skipping. I'm alone with Ross Kenner! In a limo! What should I say?

He reaches over and pats my knee. I nearly squeak—but only nearly. His hand feels as big as a baseball glove. Also warm.

"Can't get over how you two kids are all grown up." His hand is still there. As if he has forgotten. "This dress," he says, "was made with you in mind."

One finger taps the hem. A few inches above my knee. This is about to be weird. My thigh is sort of trembling.

"The dress belongs to Plum," I say.

"Then steal it!" he says, laughing.

The car pulls over. We're at my house.

I turn to say, *Thank you so much*, but he's staring at me. And suddenly my words are stuck in my throat.

"How'd you turn out so sweet?" he says.

He takes my chin in his hand. *Oh my god, for real?* One second, he's looking at me close up. Amber flecks in hazel-green eyes. The next second, my own eyes are shut. His mouth is on my mouth. Softly, as if he's testing. And then...I don't know what to call it. Not pushy or rough. Just...sexy? His tongue and my tongue meet. I feel this crazy rush. Chills. Burning chills. Every bit of me is part of this kiss.

It's so *hot*.

Then my brain kicks in. Whoa! I pull away. Try to breathe. Oh my god. Oh my god.

This is Plum's *dad*.

Chapter Eight

I'm out of the car in a heartbeat.

What, what, *what* just happened?

Ross kissed me. I was kissing him back. It lasted, what? Seven seconds? Seven really hot seconds.

But such a dumb move.

I fumble my bag. It drops to the sidewalk. Ross is already beside me, picking it up. The driver's door opens. *A little late*, I think. But then, *Oh shit! What if he could see through that black glass?*

I start up the walk, brain spinning. And I stumble. Ross grabs my hand to steady me.

"You okay?"

Am I okay? What am I? Shivering. Wobbly. His other hand is on my back. My lower back. Like a heating pad through my dress. Plum's dress. *Oh god. Plum.*

"All good." I pull away. Use my feet to walk straight. My lips are still tingling.

Ross Kenner just kissed me.

I'm on the bottom step of the porch when the door opens.

"Hi, Mom."

"I saw the limo," she says.

Thank you, inventor of tinted windows!

"Hello, Patty," Ross says. Voice like honey. "Just seeing your lovely daughter safely home. How are *you?*" He says it as if her well-being really matters to him.

"I'm fine." She is brisk but not unfriendly.

There's a second where they just look at each other. Then it's two seconds that turn into three.

"I'm tired." I move past my mother. "Thanks, Ross. That was amazing."

Oh crap, does he think I mean the kiss?

"The food!" I add. "Delicious! That artichoke."

Shut up, shut up.

I go inside, but I don't close the door all the way. He's still here. But they're talking too quietly. I can't hear them. Is he saying something about me? What was that look about?

I climb the stairs to my room. Shut the door. Throw myself on the bed. A raft in a raging storm. Oh. My. God. Did that just happen?

Ross Kenner. And me, Maya Delaney.

In the back of an actual limousine. A smoking-hot kiss.

But! Plum's *dad*! What was I thinking?

Nothing at all, clearly. I'm an idiot. And what was *he* thinking?

Did he...*does* he think I'm pretty? Do. Not. Go. There!

He's old. But still. So hot. My mouth is kind of still feeling his. Like, that's what a real kiss is supposed to be? Sean Hayden and Kevin Ho have a *lot* to learn! My only two kissers so far. Not counting my first ever, at the middle-school Halloween dance. Ben Ahmed in the haunted house. His lips were fuzzy, like the fake spiders dangling in the fake cobwebs.

And number four is Ross Kenner, lead singer for The Scratch. No pressure!

Did I suck? I hope I was okay.

Maybe he sucked at kissing too, when he was a teenager. How many girls did he kiss before Talia? She says they were dating from when they were Plum's and my age. Did they figure it out together, how kissing and stuff should work? How many girls has he kissed *since* Talia? Probably hundreds, maybe more. Maybe he's an addict. Maybe he played around when he was still married to Talia. Was that the reason for the breakup? Not because Talia got offers from other bands. Not because going on tour was hard with a kid. Maybe he kissed too many girls in the back of limousines. Maybe I'm just one more. So will that be it? The only time?

With his daughter's best friend.

If anyone else on the planet had kissed me tonight—*anyone*—I would be texting Plum right now. But she is the very last person I can tell. The thought is like a cup of cold water thrown in my face.

Cold water! Yes! I tiptoe to the bathroom. There's a light under Mom's door. I turn on the tap full force. I splash my face over and over.

My hair is damp. My top is soaked. There's a puddle on the floor.

My mother is knocking at the door.

I grab a towel. I pat dry and open the door. I keep patting. Most of my face is covered. What if a person's lips turned green when they've been kissed? Mine would be the color of a bright spring lawn.

"What's up?" I mumble through the towel.

"I was going to ask you the same thing," Mom says.

I shrug. "Just tired."

"Two nights out in a row," she says.

"You're right." She loves when I say that. "Maybe it was too much."

There's a text from Plum when I get back to my phone.

kind of sick of ross, it says.

you're still going to studio tomorrow, aren't u? I write.

I guess. but he's a clueless dad.

And I'm the worst friend she could have.

Chapter Nine

I wait till morning to text back. Not that I sleep. Not for even as long as it took for Ross to kiss me.

Have a fab day!!! I say. **Lmk if you're done in time for wings.**

I have swim-team practice on Fridays after school. Then we all go for wings. Hopefully Plum won't come—and I won't have to look her in the face. Will I ever be able to again? Even looking at Plum will feel like lying. Do. Not. Think. About. That.

Right now I have to get moving. If I'm late, Mom will ban me from going out on school nights forever.

Alone at the corner table at lunch, I unwrap my cheese sandwich. Ross Kenner pops into my head for the hundredth time. For the hundredth time, I blink hard. Twice.

"Got something in your eye?" Jones plunks himself down across from me. There are new photos online, he reports. Inside Hot Sam's. Plum and me and Ross, edging through the bar.

"What's he like?" Jones whispers. "For real?"

The bite of cheddar and bread goes dry as dust in my mouth. I shrug. Pretend to chew. Finally swallow.

"He's just Plum's dad," I say.

On my way to life skills class, my phone hums.

A text.

Hi, this is Eddie, your new pal from the Scratch team. Got this number from your mom. Ross asked me to connect with you—maybe you want to visit the

studio this afternoon to hear Plum sing? lmk. cheers.

My body prickles as if I've swallowed ants. I mean, Ross wants to see me again?

I blush, feeling an echo of the kiss on my mouth. Ross didn't tell Eddie, did he? Or was the kiss so nothing to him that he forgot it happened?

I glance down to see what I'm wearing. Jeans and my frumpy gray sweater. Not exactly ideal for visiting a recording studio.

And! Main obstacle. *No way* could I be in a room with Plum and Ross together. That would be...the kiss of death. Pun intended. It would be like cheating on my friendship with Plum.

Sorry, big test at school, I type. **Thanks tho.**

In life skills, I hand in my dumb vision board. We had to cut out pictures from magazines to show our "hopes and dreams." Poor Ms. DaSilva. This is not her path to success with teenagers. Her nickname is Saliva.

My hopes and dreams include a fake fur coat and a swimming pool, lit at night.

"I'm surprised that you had time to do your homework, Maya." Ms. DaSilva peers at my board. "Going out to bars at your age."

I wish I had a snappy comeback. The best I can do is, "I was helping Plum pursue her dream of a better relationship with her father."

Was I, though? Or have I sabotaged that forever? It's all I can think about till the bell rings. I know one thing for sure. Not one person would be happy to hear about what happened last night. Not Plum and not her mother. Not *my* mother, that's for sure. Maybe Ava would be thrilled.

The good news is that none of them will ever know. The bad news is that I'm stuck holding it. This giant secret is all mine. If I can't tell Plum, it shouldn't have happened.

"Earth to Maya. Hello?" Ava waves a hand in front

of my face. I'm standing like a dolt next to the water fountain.

"Go ahead," Ava says. "Drinks are on me."

"Very funny." But I lean down and take a long drink.

"So is it weird to hang out with somebody famous?" says Ava. "Like a fangirl?"

"I'm not a fangirl, Ava. I'm Plum's friend!" *Yeah, but for how long?*

"Is her dad as hot as he looks on YouTube?" Ava asks.

"What?" One horrible second ticks by. She couldn't know! My fear must sound like outrage. She puts up her hands, like, whoa!

"Hey! No offense! I just mean, you know. Think about what *my* dad would look like in leather pants!"

I have to laugh. Ava's dad is a nice tubby dentist. He hides his belly under a white medical jacket. What would *my* dad look like in leather pants? And how would I feel if my dad kissed Plum? He never would, obviously. He's not a rock star. He has probably never been inside a limo. He has definitely never been alone with Plum. And she would never, ever, ever let him kiss her.

We go into world events. Last class of the week. And yay, we get to watch YouTube videos. Protests in Iran against the mistreatment of women. People with real problems.

Now only swim team before the day is over. Plum hasn't texted all day. I hope that means she's having fun. What excuse can I drum up if Eddie mentions the big test I'm supposedly having? Lying to Plum feels so wrong. But is it worse than telling the truth?

I hate this!

My phone dings. My mother.

Call me please.

Well, that can wait.

Coach is fierce about being on time. I go straight from class to the changeroom. Most of the other swimmers are senior girls. I know them from the pool and that's all. On a normal day, they ignore me. Today a couple of them look at me twice. Leftover fame from the photos at Hot Sam's.

I'm in my suit and poolside before anyone else. Coach Franks nods hello and points to the list of warm-ups on the whiteboard. This is where I get to be just me. Safe from prying eyes. We're doing eggbeaters, no hands, for four minutes. Ripping up and down the pool, freestyle. Three strokes, breath. Five strokes, breath. Seven strokes, breath.

Then Coach makes us do one-on-one sprints. Life is all about the stop clock. It's easy to go faster if someone is racing in the next lane. My brain is so happy to stop thinking. No Ross, no kiss, no being a shitty friend. My arms and legs take over.

I win the first heat. And then the second, against Lindsey Bowen. I am a churning monster. Coach puts me in with Suzie Frye, the fastest girl on the team.

At the end of the lane, I'm three strokes ahead. I look at the clock. I beat my own record! Suzie is staring at me, like, what just happened? She starts to laugh. We high-five.

"Whatever you had for breakfast, Maya," says Coach, "have it again tomorrow."

He tells us all to use the kickboard for four lengths. Then a slow freestyle to cool down. On my third turn, Plum comes out of the changeroom.

Lindsey is right behind me. I can't pause. I keep kicking, head down. What is Plum doing here? She is wearing street shoes. Bad idea. Coach waves his arms. Jabs a finger at her Blundstones.

I keep the pace going. Do a flip turn at the wall. On my next breath, Plum has backed up to the changeroom door. She's pointing at the pool, at me. Coach is shaking his head.

I keep swimming. Next breath, Plum's hands are up as if she's arguing. What the eff is going on? Next breath, the changeroom door is closing behind her.

Coach taps the clipboard against his leg. A few more turns, and he blows the whistle.

We hoist ourselves out of the pool. We grab our towels. I'm not cold. But I'm shivering. I'm nearly at the changeroom door.

"Maya?" Coach says.

Uh-oh. I turn. "Yes, Coach?"

"Plum Kenner came by. She says it's urgent."

"What is?"

Coach nods his head about five times. "Exactly," he says. "Urgent and top secret. You tell her, next time, she takes off her shoes."

"Okay, Coach."

All I can think is that something really, *really* crap has happened.

Did Ross...did he tell her?

Chapter Ten

She was upset enough to interrupt swim team. But when I get to the changeroom, Plum is gone.

I peel out of my suit and jump in a hot shower. The other girls are mostly dressed when I finish. I rub the towel so hard across my back, my skin nearly comes off.

Girls are saying, "Bye, have a great weekend!" Lindsey and Suzie compare the weight of their swim bags. I'm still in my underwear.

"Maya?" Ava is standing beside the wet-towel bin.

"Oh, hi." My stomach turns over. Ava never comes to meet me. Especially here. "Have you seen Plum?" I say. "Did she say how the day went with her dad?"

"Have you looked at your phone?" Ava says.

"Uh, not yet."

I try to play it cool. *What's on my phone?* Ava waits while I drag on my jeans. Her phone case is leather with fake brass studs. I see Suzie check her phone and sneak a look at Lindsey.

I pull on my tee, as if I don't care. Then my sweater. Lindsey and Suzie slide to the door.

"Bye, My," they say. Not quite normal.

Ava taps her foot. She knows I'm being slow on purpose.

"Let's go." I grab my backpack. "Where's Plum?"

We're in the hallway. We push through the double doors into the yard. Jones is leaning against the flagpole.

"Where's Plum?" I ask again.

"She went home," says Jones.

"Home? No wings?" They always wait for me to finish swim team.

"I don't blame her," Ava says.

"What the hell, Ava?" She's pissing me off.

"Maya," says Jones. "Have you seen it yet?" He turns to Ava. "Has she seen it?"

Ava shakes her head. "She won't look."

"Look at what?" My hand goes to my pocket.

"You probably should," says Jones.

"I'm not *not* looking," I say, pretending. Could they please vanish in a puff of black smoke?

I take out my phone. I don't have to look far. Alerts fill my screen. From social media. From so-called friends.

A text from my mother. The preview says **Had a call from Talia about**

I ignore that and skip to a text from Plum: **wtf?**

All the noise is about a photo. Not one I've seen before. It's a bit dark, a bit blurry. The photographer did not use a flash. It takes me a second—but only a second—to figure it out. I know that yellow porch light.

We're in front of my house. Me and Ross Kenner. Ross Kenner and me.

Not inside the limousine. I shudder in relief. But I can see why Plum might've bolted.

Ava gives a little laugh. "See?" she says. "The secret's out."

I want to slap her phone out of her hand. I'd love to hear the nasty crack when it hits the sidewalk. My head is humming. Like an old fan doing its best to stay cool.

"Maya?" says Jones. Very softly.

The photo shows the moment when I lost my balance. Ross is grabbing my wrist and his hand is at my back. Actually, it's pretty close to cupping my butt. Now that I see it, I remember the heat of his hand. Right through my dress. But that was a second later. And higher, near my hip. In the photo, I don't think he's even really touching me.

It does *not* show the kiss! The secret is *not* out.

I glance up at Jones and Ava. They're both waiting. Little do they know.

I am so, so lucky. This can be explained.

"What?" I say. "I tripped. Ross tried to catch me. It's not what it looks like."

"I told you, Ava!" says Jones. "No way would Maya hook up with—"

"*What?*" I say. "Your mind is in the gutter, Ava."

But I kind of did, didn't I? My neck grows warm. I feel the imprint of Ross's mouth on my mouth. This time it doesn't feel so good.

"Who took the picture?" Ava says.

When did Ava become someone I have to answer to?

"I'm guessing the driver," I say. "He was a dick."

"He should be fired," says Jones.

"It's all over the internet," says Ava. "Hashtag MeToo, big-time. People are going nuts."

Jones grabs Ava's arm. Tells her to shush.

I slip my phone into my pocket. "I have to—" My mind is a jumble of things that I have to do. I have to ignore what Ava is saying. I have to not care that a photo of me is suddenly viral. A misleading photo. Oh my god. I have to think of what to tell my mother. This is for sure why she texted. So Talia must know too!

And Plum.

I want to crawl under a blanket.

First I have to get away from Jones and Ava. I need to find Plum. No wonder she stomped onto the pool deck wearing street shoes.

"I can't come for wings tonight," I say. "I have a...a thing."

I turn to go. I walk away like a normal person. I want them to think I'm okay. But the instant I'm out of sight, I start to run.

I betrayed my friend. I let the kiss happen and didn't think about her until after. And then some dumb driver tricked me. The whole world thinks I'm a slutty groupie.

I have to see Plum. I have to tell her. Not what I told Ava. Even though I really did trip. But Plum—and Plum alone—has to know what happened before Fred took the photo. Effing Fred. If I can't tell Plum about the kiss, it will be a black hole between us.

Hot tears fill my eyes. I'm still running. I just have to get to Plum. Into her room with the bluebird wallpaper. Night-light shaped like a mushroom. Window shades made of bamboo. Giant pillows like pink clouds.

I will tell her everything.

Right. Now.

I turn the corner onto Shaw Avenue. And stop short. My pits are damp, my cheeks burn. I duck behind the fat old tree on Mr. Arnott's lawn, next door to Plum's house.

A taxi sits at the curb. Ross Kenner is standing on the doorstep.

Chapter Eleven

Oh god, oh god, oh god. Now what?

I pray that Ross can't hear me trying to catch my breath. But I can hear him knocking. Plum's house doesn't have a porch. The door is just a step up from the walk. The garden is full of flowering bushes in the summer. Now the leaves are fading to yellow.

Did Ross come in a taxi because he'll never trust a limo driver again? Is he here to explain the photo to his darling daughter?

Is Plum even in there?

I check the Find My app on the phone. Yes, Plum is inside. Her icon overlaps with the little blue dot that shows me. Her room is at the back. She's too chill to sneak a look from behind a curtain. And she is *not* coming to the door.

I text, **it's your dad knocking, not me**. In case she's also checking Find My and sees my icon next to hers. **i'm hiding behind Arnott's tree.**

I edge my face around the trunk of the tree. Ross knocks again. He puts a hand on the doorknob. Locked. He glances at the row of clay pots on the windowsill. He reaches over a shrub in the front garden. He lifts the third pot from the left.

I guess it's not a surprise that Ross knows where they keep the spare key. He might be the one who chose that place. But it's kind of rude, isn't it? Since he hasn't lived here in six years.

As if my brainwaves zap into his head, he puts the key back. I duck out of sight in case he turns around. I would faint with shame if he saw me. He'd think I'm stalking him.

I text her again. **Plum, pretty please can we talk?**

Nothing.

I'm ignoring every message from Jones. I am not looking at any site that has a picture I don't want to see. I truly do not want to know what anyone is saying.

tree to Plum, I text. **good thing Mr. Arnott is blind.**

My phone buzzes. For a second I expect to see Plum saying *ha ha*. But it's my mother.

I know swim team is over. Please call me.

Not a chance. Not till I've talked with Plum.

A car slows down, coming the other way. It's Talia. Good thing she didn't arrive from behind me. I must look like an idiot, lurking by the tree. Talia's old Honda pulls into the driveway. Music spills out the open window. The engine goes off. The music dies.

"What are you doing here?" Talia's voice is loud and clear. Has she seen me? I press myself against the bark. Her car door shuts. Almost a slam.

"Hear me out!" Ross says.

Phew! It's Ross she's pissed at, not me. I risk a peek. Talia is hugging a tote bag against her chest. Body-language defense.

"Hang on," says Ross. "I'll pay the taxi."

"Just leave," says Talia.

I hear the cab drive off. Ross must have thrown money through the window.

"I want to talk to Plum," he says. "But she won't answer the door."

"I guess that means she doesn't want to talk to you." Talia is so mad. "No means no, remember? Number one lesson we taught our daughter?"

They're at the top of the path. Right outside the door. I inch around the tree to stay out of sight.

Plum may not be answering my texts, but I can guarantee she's reading them.

your mom is here, I write.

"I don't want to talk to you either." Talia's voice has gone up. "You make me sick. That's Plum's best friend you—"

I close my eyes, stomach in a sick knot.

"Talia! It's not what—"

"I suppose you think she looks like her mother."

"I never!" Ross shouts. "The kid tripped over a crack in the walk! The dick of a driver—"

I want to run away. But if I move, they'll see me. I'm stuck where I am, the word *kid* buzzing in my ears. Being a kid didn't seem to matter when he was kissing me!

she's coming inside, I text.

I think how awful it is for Plum to hear them fighting. I *have* to talk to her first. Explain. Tell the truth. Even if it's the very last thing I ever get to say to her.

"I don't want to talk to you," Talia says again.

"Better inside than out here," says Ross.

they're BOTH coming in! I add.

"Plum is my daughter too," says Ross.

"When did you remember that?" snaps Talia.

Finally a series of texts comes back.

k, I'm outta here, says Plum.

Back way

Meet me in 5

She doesn't have to say where.

I peek around the tree. Ross is holding open the door for Talia. She squeezes past as if he's toxic. Then click. They're inside.

I launch myself onto the sidewalk. Around Mr. Arnott's corner lot. Up his driveway to the garage. Mr. Arnott's daughter sold his car a few years ago when his bad eyesight meant he couldn't drive. We're too old for forts, but it's kind of our fort. Ms. Arnott even gave us a couch from their basement and an old striped blanket.

Plum is already here. She's wearing the blanket. Her hair is stuffed under a woolly hat. I'm flooded with hope just seeing her. She's watching her house through the little cracked window.

"I barely got out in time," she says. "Didn't even grab a jacket." She doesn't look at me.

Come on. Look at me.

"Not sure she won't kill him," she says. "*I'm* so mad I want to smash something." Not a comfort that there's a window two inches away.

I'm waiting for Plum to scream at me. Then I'll explain. Apologize. Grovel. Promise anything.

I take a big breath. Plum whips her head around to look at me.

"This is messed up," she says. "So you'd better tell me. What exactly happened with the skeezebag formerly known as my father?"

Chapter Twelve

"You're not mad at me?" I say.

"Should I be?" says Plum.

"It's just...when you didn't answer my texts—"

"I was in the shower! Trying to calm down about Ross! And I get out and you're lurking behind a tree like a lunatic and my parents are bursting through the front door."

"A shower?" I start to laugh. All that freaking out for nothing. Except it's not nothing.

"You better tell me what happened," Plum says.

Big breath. Okay. This is the moment. Tell the truth.

"We dropped you off," I begin. "He got back in the car. He sat next to me. Where you were sitting before. Instead of across."

"Ew," says Plum. "Why?"

This is hard. *Because he was going to kiss me.* In my head, I see me from his point of view. A fangirl in a too-short skirt. A fangirl slightly tipsy on prosecco. A fangirl waiting in the back of his limo. I shrug.

"He, um, said something about..."

Plum is watching me so closely, her eyes might pierce my skin.

"He said 'nice dress' or something, and I said it was yours. And then—"

Oh my god, it was such a cheesy line. I didn't see it that way last night. "He said, um..."

This is awful. "He said, 'How'd you get to be so sweet?'"

Plum barks out a yelp of disgust. “And then what?”

I put my hands over my eyes. “I’m not sure I can look at you while I’m saying this.”

She lets out a noisy sigh. But she turns back to the window.

And I tell her.

As the words come out of my mouth, I know it wasn’t my fault. I wasn’t waiting for a kiss. It happened *to* me. There’s a reason girls say “he hit on me.” It’s kind of like being hit.

Five seconds of the deadest silence.

“A kiss?” she says. “Or a peck?”

“A kiss,” I say. “On the mouth.”

“Like, how long?”

How *long*?

She starts to count. “One, two, three, done? Or one. Two. Three. Four—”

“Plum, stop.” She doesn’t need to know seven. She really doesn’t.

"Did you scream? *I'm* going to scream."

I shake my head. "I just kind of—" I shiver. I close my eyes. I grope for an imaginary door handle. "I got out. I ran up the walk. That's when I tripped. When the photo was taken. Ross was following me."

"My father is a predator!" Plum's fury is loud and certain. "Why aren't you pissed?" she says. "You must still be in shock. Where's the rage? You were *assaulted*!"

"Assaulted?" It didn't feel like an assault. But was it? I'm so confused. Am I a victim? A victim is weak and pathetic, right? I don't want to be a victim. So how do we name it?

Because there's one thing I don't tell Plum. Since it won't help anyone to say it out loud. I want to forget it myself.

I didn't ask for that kiss.

But it was nice.

Better than nice. It was the hottest—

Stop! The quality of the kiss isn't the point. The point is that I'm sixteen. Ross is more than twice my age. He did something wrong, not me. No matter who he is.

Right?

Do I believe that? Yes.

I look at Plum. She's watching me. As if she can see the wheels turning.

"It's SO GROSS!" Plum hurls the words.

"It *is* gross," I whisper. Gross. Even creepy.

Deeply creepy.

I take a breath and shake it off. "So. Enough of that." Because the kiss is not actually what the trouble's about. "There are two parts to this."

"What do you mean?"

"The first part is your dad...you know, kissing me."

"So slimy I'm done thinking about it," Plum says.

"But nobody knows, right?" I say. "Only three people in the world. You, me and—"

"And my pig of a father." Plum glares.

I nod. "And none of us is ever going to tell another person."

For sure I won't. Plum won't either. As for Ross—

"Ross will deny it to his dying day," says Plum. "So yeah. Forget about the kiss. Toss it into a dumpster."

"Yeah, but the much bigger problem," I say, "is that I'm an internet slut."

"So true!" she says, almost laughing. "There are photos to prove it. More than just what the driver took. We were hanging out in a bar. You were wearing a really short skirt. There were fans and paparazzi. Total set-up for victim-blaming. *Of course* the rock star had his hand on your butt. You were obviously asking for it."

"I tripped." The truth sounds like a feeble excuse.

"And who's going to believe that? Ross is being blasted online." Plum starts reading from her phone. "'What a lech!' 'Such a tragedy that my hero turns out to be a creep.' Not wrong there," Plum sticks in. "Though 'tragedy' is stretching it."

She scrolls some more. "Here's another one. 'He should have his balls burned off.' See? They've started posting pictures of other girls with him. Like, fifty other girls since The Scratch began. There's a gif of his hand on guitar strings that turn out to be a bra strap. And you're getting your share too."

"I am?"

"Are you being dense on purpose? All those cameras at Hot Sam's the other night? We're *in high school*, Maya! Hardly anyone knows I'm his kid. He only acts like I'm his kid when he's bored and wants to text!"

My phone vibrates and goes *ping-ping*.

My mother. **Call me right now!**

"My mom must have heard something."

"Oh god." Plum winces. "Our mothers. They'll kill him."

"Plum, promise me that—"

"Don't worry. I would never tell her. Never."

"Till the end of time, right? Not yours and not mine."

"No kidding. I'd rather die," says Plum. "Because this one shitty kiss would kill them. Seriously."

My phone rings.

Mom.

I decline to answer. We have to figure out what to do.

"If we put the kiss in the dumpster, like you said..." I begin. "It's really only a photo. His hand is, you know—it looks inappropriate. But not criminal. I don't think it even touched me."

Plum sits down on the couch and jumps right back up. "Ow! Cold!"

"You want my jacket for a bit?"

She shakes her head. Checks her phone. I push my phone into my pocket.

"Not looking won't make it go away," says Plum. "It's out of control. Have you *met* the internet?"

I lean against the wall. My whole body wants to groan.

"Ava must be in heaven," I say.

Plum laughs out loud for the first time. "Too right. She's loving this."

A noise makes us jump. Hinges creak as the door opens.

"Thought I might find you here." Plum's mother. My heart stops.

"I want you inside," she says. "Now. Stuff to discuss." She sounds like a teacher rounding up kids after recess.

Plum obeys by shrugging off the blanket.

"Plum, no jacket? Have I raised a ninny?"

No one says what we have to discuss. We all know. I have this brain flash. *Plum's mother and I have kissed the same man.* I squeeze my eyes hard shut. Nobody knows about the kiss.

I say it again and again inside my head. Nobody knows about the kiss. This is about a dumb photo. A dumb photo taken by a dumb driver with dumb-luck timing. I can legit say that Ross's hand never touched my butt.

Nobody knows about the kiss.

Chapter Thirteen

Nearly back at the house, Talia speaks.

"You said you were going to visit the studio today, Plum. You did not mention that you were going to sing."

Plum winces. "How did you—"

"I had a call from Bella. She's a vulture. She wants to sign you up."

"Oh jeez," says Plum. "No way."

"That's what I told her," Talia says. "No rush to mess up your life."

"Where did Ross go?" Plum asks as we reach her door.

Talia's head snaps around. She gives Plum a look. "You saw him here? You were hiding?"

"Duh," says Plum. "So where did he go?"

"Probably driving around in circles," Talia says. "He won't give up until you forgive him."

"As if," says Plum. "I'm blocking his texts."

Inside, Talia puts a pan of oat milk on the stove. I pull out my phone.

"Umm..." I clear my throat. "I guess I should call my—"

"Your mother is on her way over," says Talia. She stirs cocoa powder and raw sugar into the milk. "You can't disappear and not expect to be looked for." She turns to scowl at us. "You are loved, after all."

I squirm. Plum sends me a laser-beam message with her eyeballs: *We are sworn to eternal secrecy.*

I nod, but—Mom is coming over? Things are *way* out of our control.

Headlights brighten the room for a second. When did it get dark? A taxi is pulling into the drive. One of the kitchen windows looks out that way.

Not my mom. We're only three blocks from here.

"Eddie," says Plum.

Another taxi is at the curb.

"And *Bella*?"

"No way to avoid Bella," says Plum's mother. "Moments like this are made for managers." She goes to open the front door.

"Come on in," she says. As if it's a party. "Oh hi, Patty. Good timing." We hear Talia tell my mom, "Yup, the kids are here." She makes introductions in the hallway.

"Team Ross takes over," Plum whispers. She stirs the cocoa while we consult.

"I feel sick." Maybe because my mother is about to walk into the room. She doesn't come to Plum's house too often. She's not quite cool enough to still be best friends with Talia.

“We just have to stick to the new story,” says Plum.

“The only story,” I say. “The truth.” Just missing a few key details.

“Right.”

“Maya!” Mom throws her arms around me. Then, “Why didn’t you answer my texts?” I bet she really wants to yell. Lucky for me, other people are nearby. Eddie and Bella come in with Talia. They say hello. They make hugging motions. The kitchen feels a little crowded. Talia tells everyone to sit in the living room. She offers wine. All the women want wine. Eddie opts for hot chocolate with us.

“I have a call in to Kristy Glenn.” Bella plunks into the best chair. “She’s in a play in New York. Best to get her onside up front. The press could push her to say the wrong thing.”

“Not hard with her,” Eddie mutters.

“Maya.” Mom uses her soft, caring voice. “Can you tell us what happened?”

“Good place to start.” Eddie makes heavy-duty eye contact with me. “You okay?”

I guess he means, am I suffering trauma? Four adults are staring. I don’t know where to look. Not at my mother, obviously.

“It’s probably best if we hear the truth,” Talia says. Not meanly. A statement of fact. Her calm is why Plum doesn’t usually lie to her mother. Except about eating french fries nearly every day. My neck starts to sweat. How many girls did Ross kiss during their marriage? How many confessed to his wife?

Plum’s eyes say, *Tell no one.* They also say, *You’ve got this.*

“Not really sure why everyone’s so edgy,” I begin, laughing a little. I sound nervous. I take a breath. “I am totally fine! I tripped on the path. The asshole driver—sorry, Mom, but clearly he is one. He took a photo. But it wasn’t like that. I mean, Ross’s hand looks kind of wrong, I know. But I don’t think he touched me. A split second maybe. Him reaching out after I tripped. Nothing weird." Am I babbling? Another breath. "What's weird is now. Us sitting here. The photo going viral. *This* stuff."

Do they all exhale at the same time? Or is it only me? Plum gives me a teeny tiny thumbs-up.

"Oh, Maya," says my mother. "We needed to hear from you about what happened. To make sure that... that no line was crossed."

She's being so careful. No one says out loud what they're worried about. Because Plum is in the room? Ha. They don't know how quickly Plum jumped straight to *my dad is a predator*!

"I can see why all the attention seems unfair." Mom is still talking. "But Ross is famous, and you're a young—"

"I'm just mad at the driver who took the picture," I say. "*He* was the sleaze."

"He was fired about eleven minutes after he sold it," Eddie says.

"Good!" says Plum. "I can't believe anyone pays for crap like that."

"Meet the real world," Bella says.

"So what do we do?" Talia is leaning against the doorframe. "Or, I should say, what do *you* do, Bella? Eddie? To fix this."

"Yes, what's the plan?" says my mother. "I don't want my daughter's name out there."

"Too late for that." Bella waves her phone. "Maya has been identified."

I close my eyes. My face, my butt, my name, all over the internet.

"We have to do two things," Eddie says. I open my eyes and pay attention.

"Here comes rescue mode," murmurs Plum.

"First—" Eddie begins.

"A statement," Bella interrupts.

Eddie ignores her. "First, Ross issues a statement," he says. "Crafted by me. Maybe with a 'no big deal' quote from Maya? And at the same time, we throw something out there to make people look the other way."

Bella is nodding her head. "Totally agree. A diversion."

"Like what?" says Plum. "What could be worse than this? Please don't make him marry Kristy Glenn."

Talia snorts. Actually snorts. Doom to Kristy Glenn.

"Could it be a good surprise instead of a bad one?" I say. Without any idea of what that might be. "Like, about the new album?"

Eddie is gazing at Talia. "I don't suppose...?"

Talia sighs. "I want to say no way," she says. Her eyes are as hard as concrete. "I want to bite his head off. But he's Plum's dad. And this is public. Maya is out there flapping in the wind. So I'll hear what you're thinking."

Eddie takes a breath. Mom puts up her hand. Her eyes bounce between Plum and me.

"Do the girls need to be here? Maybe it's a little much?"

"Mom!" Why does she treat me like I'm six years old?

But Plum springs to her feet. "Right!" She pulls me up. "We'll go for a walk while our futures are decided by concerned adults."

She drags me into the hall. We grab our jackets. Plum rams her arms into the sleeves. I sling mine around my neck like a scarf. We bolt through the door. It shuts with a bang behind us. For a second we hang on to each other. Then it seems funny. We run, laughing, across the lawn. We turn the corner. A taxi is pulling away.

Plum's dad is standing right in front of us.

Chapter Fourteen

"Plum!" Ross opens his arms wide. As if she's running toward a hug from her father.

She stops dead. I do too.

Ross is grinning. "Bella was so excited to hear you sing today—"

Plum makes a choking sound. His smile falters. His arms drop.

Plum is crying. Suddenly seeing the villain, I guess. I slide my arm over her shoulder. She was singing with him only a few hours ago. And now her dad has turned into...what? Maybe he always *was* this guy. We're just face-to-face with it for the first time. All week she has given him extra chances. But today, because he kissed the wrong girl, it's a big ugly mess.

"Plum? Honey?"

"Don't you *dare* call me honey!" Plum explodes.

Ross looks at me. "Maya, can you give us a minute alone to—"

Plum shakes her head no and takes in a shuddering breath.

"I can't even look at your face!" She spits it out. "And I don't want to see you again until you grow up and own your crap." She darts past and keeps running.

Ross watches for a second, but he doesn't try to catch her. He turns back to me.

"She means it," I say.

"What did you tell her?" Ross says.

I see Plum dash up the Arnott driveway. I know where to find her.

"I told her what the photo didn't show. The truth about what happened before."

"And what truth is that?" he asks.

As if we get to choose.

A second later I know that we do. Truth comes in lots of little pieces. Collected facts and points of view. But in this moment, only one fact matters.

"Plum is mad at you," I say. "For lots of reasons. Not just because you kissed me. Which you shouldn't have. I'm sixteen. You know that, right? But also, you went away. You got busy. You talk to her, but you don't really listen. You live in Berlin. She's way down the list of people you care about. Turns out you're a really shitty dad. Proof of that is kissing your daughter's best friend."

It pours out. But now what do I do? How do I make my dramatic exit? Duck around him and follow Plum? Or turn my back and retreat?

His famous eyes look right into mine for a second.

Like he's on a poster. Then he flinches and shrugs. He jams both fists into his pockets.

"Are they all in there?" he says. He tips his chin in the general direction of Plum's house. "Planning the big cover-up?"

"Nobody knows about the kiss," I say. "Except Plum. We won't tell, and you better not either. But yeah, they're all there. Dealing with the dumb photo."

He nods and slinks past me. Like a little kid in trouble. Eddie and Bella will fix his life. He'll do what they say. Until the next time.

I yell after him, "If you mess up again, Plum will never forgive you."

I stand there, feeling kind of tall, until he's gone. Then I run to find Plum in the garage. Her eyes are red, but she's not crying anymore. She's curled up on the cold, damp sofa. I sink down next to her.

"What a jerk," she says.

I tell her what I said to him. She puts her head on my shoulder. We sit there till we're freezing.

"No way is he still there," says Plum. We figure it's safe to go back.

It's a party inside. Like us goofing around after an exam. They've ordered pizza. Opened another bottle of wine. They fill us in on the plan.

"We wrote a statement for Ross to give," Eddie says. "He'll say the girl is a friend of his daughter. Crack in the sidewalk. Awkward angle. No big deal." He turns to me. "The next couple of days will be a bit crazy," he says. "Rumors will fly around. More gossip. A few snide remarks. But it will fade, I promise. It really will."

"And Talia has offered—" begins Bella.

"Talia did not *offer*," says Talia. "But Talia has agreed—"

"To record a song for the new Scratch album!" Bella does not try to hide her glee about this.

Plum looks horrified. Which is how I feel. Talia is doing this for me. Coming out of retirement to play music with a man she doesn't like too much anymore.

Talia puts an arm around each of us.

"It's okay," she says. "I'm not thrilled that he seems to always get what he wants. But I could use some cash. And it's a song *I* wrote. Called 'Time for You to Go Away.'"

I start to laugh.

"Really?" Plum is laughing too.

"We'll push for it to be the single," says Bella.

"Talia," I say. "This is beyond huge. I don't know what to say!"

"I'm doing it for me too," she says. "It could pay to start a little music school. In a place outside the living room! Make the comeback worthwhile."

When it's time to go, I hug Plum. For a long time.

"You're the best," she whispers.

On the walk home, Mom starts to talk.

"Something happened to me," she says. "Maybe ten years ago? A little more, I guess." Wind blows her hair, and she pushes it off her face. "With Ross."

My feet stop moving. "What do you mean?"

She takes my arm, as if I'm the old lady.

"It was a summer night," she says. "July."

She keeps talking while I take it in. A backyard barbecue. Friends and neighbors. Lots of laughter. Lots of wine. A kiss in the kitchen while cleaning up. Over in a moment.

We're walking slowly. Mom's voice has slowed down too.

"Talia knew somehow. She said it happened so many times she lost count. Random women. And she always knew."

I'm not even breathing.

Until I say, "That's nuts."

And Mom says, "Yeah. So if you ever want to talk–" She stops. We walk along, arm in arm. Maybe she secretly knows my secret. Maybe Talia does too. But for now it's mine.

Maybe in ten years I'll tell her the real story.

That time, I'll say, when I tripped on the path? When Plum's dad tried to steady me? And the photo went viral? And you all freaked out?

Well, I tripped because my head was spinning. This thing happened inside the limo. This thing I hardly remember now. At the time it was a big moment. It should never have happened.

But really, it was just this one kiss.

Acknowledgements

Thank you to the whole Orca pod for letting me tackle a hi-lo book, and especially to my editor, Gabrielle Prendergast, for recognizing and helping me navigate the complexity of what can happen between the wrong two people.

If someone reading this book needs to talk about a situation that doesn't feel right, please call:

In Canada:

KidsHelpPhone

kidshelpphone.ca

call: 1-800-668-6868

text: 686868

In the USA:

Teenline

teenline.org

call: 1-800-852-8336

text: 839863

Or talk to a trusted adult such as a parent, doctor, teacher or friend.

WANT MORE FAST-PACED READS? FIND YOUR NEXT orca soundings

Nonbinary teen Brick must rescue the crew of a spaceship they snuck onto when it is taken over by pirates.

★ "Engrossing and thrilling."
—*Kirkus Reviews*

Hannah goes on a search for her younger brother, who has disappeared with their overdue rent money, and finds unexpected romance along the way.

"[A] suspenseful and heartening tale."
—*Kirkus Reviews*

Seventeen-year-old Ichiro secretly enters a drag performance contest. What will his friends say?

"Dramatic, optimistic, and emotionally engaging."
—Kirkus Reviews

When Adele is forced to spend two weeks at a youth reform camp, she has no idea it will lead to a complicated and dangerous love triangle.

"An engaging, focused romantic thriller."
—Kirkus Reviews

Marthe Jocelyn is the award-winning author and illustrator of over fifty books for babies, kids and teens. Her illustrated books have been shortlisted for both the Governor General's Literary Award and the Marilyn Baillie Picture Book Award. Her book *What We Hide* won the inaugural Amy Mathers Teen Book Award in 2014. She has also been the recipient of the prestigious Vicky Metcalf Award for her body of work. She now lives in Stratford, Ontario, with not enough bookshelves.